Groundwood Books / House of Anansi Press
110 Spadina Avenue, Suite 801, Toronto, Ontario M5V 2K4
or c/o Publishers Group West
1700 Fourth Street, Berkeley, CA 94710

We acknowledge for their financial support of our publishing program the
Government of Canada through the Canada Book Fund (CBF).

Library and Archives Canada Cataloguing in Publication

Krishnaswami, Uma
Out of the way! Out of the way! / Uma Krishnaswami ; Uma
Krishnaswamy, illustrator.
ISBN 978-1-55498-130-4
I. Uma Krishnaswamy II. Title.
PZ7.K75Ou 2012   j813'.54   C2011-906032-9

The illustrations were created with mixed media, including poster color,
watercolor, acrylic and ink.
Design by Michael Solomon
Printed and bound in China

OUT of the WAY!
OUT of the WAY!

For our fathers.

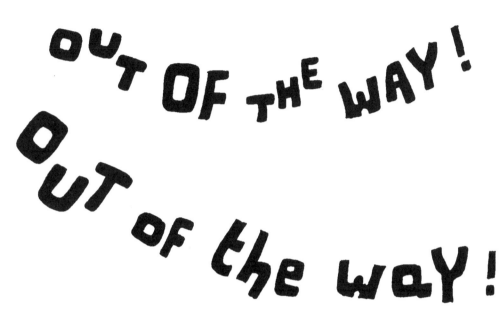

OUT OF THE WAY! OUT of the waY!

Story by Uma Krishnaswami
Pictures by Uma Krishnaswamy

Groundwood Books
House of Anansi Press
Toronto   Berkeley

A dusty path ran through a village.
People and animals
walked up and down,
going from here to there
and back again.

One day a boy spotted something
small and green in the middle of the path.

"A baby tree," he said.

He took some rocks and put them all around it.

"Hey, you!" called
a mango seller, hurrying past.

OUT OF THE WAY!
OUT of the WAY!

As the baby tree grew bigger,
the feet of all the people
going from here to there and back again
wore the path into a curving lane.

"Hey, you!" cried the bullock-cart man,
with his animals nodding their heads,
one-two, one-two.

out of the WAY!

out of the WAY!

The tree grew bigger, and bigger still.
Birds perched and chirped in its forking branches.

One day the boy saw a pair of crows
building a nest with twigs and straw and grass
and even bits of bright thread.
He called everyone to see.

Trrring! Trring! went bicycle bells.
"Hey, you!" yelled the riders.

OUT of THE way!

OUT of THE way!

The tree's trunk thickened.
Its branches spread wider, and wider still.

On their way from here to there and back again,
the boy and his friends laughed and joked
and clowned around beneath the tree,

while overhead, squirrels and parakeets
feasted on their favorite berries.

Meanwhile, the feet of all the people
and the wheels of carts and bicycles
rushing there and back again
rutted and drummed and pounded the lane
until it flowed like a river around the tree,
getting out of its way, out of its way.

OUT of THE way!

The tree's leaves grew like feathers.
Its waving branches invited children and grownups
and animals too, to meet under their spreading canopy.

As the tree became a meeting place, the street became a road.

Machines graded and flattened it,
sputtering their way carefully around the tree,
while from the highest branches,
flycatchers dashed out in hunting parties.

In time, a young man who knew this tree well crossed the road with his own small children.

"Hey, you!" yelled the riders of motorbikes and scooters. "Out of the way, out of the way!"

By the time the young man's children grew up, and he grew old...

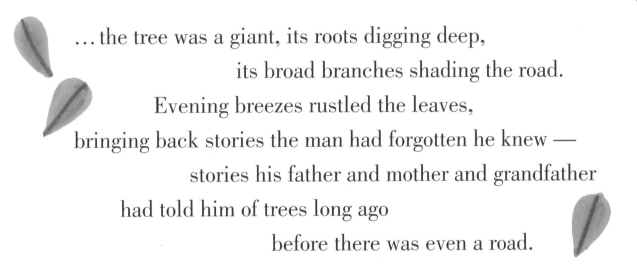

...the tree was a giant, its roots digging deep,
    its broad branches shading the road.
    Evening breezes rustled the leaves,
bringing back stories the man had forgotten he knew —
    stories his father and mother and grandfather
had told him of trees long ago
    before there was even a road.

Even today, those stories are told and retold,
as the traffic rattles past,
going from here to there and back again.

But sometimes the drivers of cars
and buses and trucks
and vans and tractors

stop and stay a while …

...and listen.